DONALD'S WILD ADVENTURE

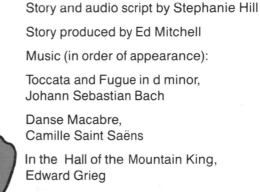

Story and audio script by Stephanie Hill

Story produced by Ed Mitchell

Music (in order of appearance):

Toccata and Fugue in d minor,
Johann Sebastian Bach

Danse Macabre,
Camille Saint Saëns

In the Hall of the Mountain King,
Edward Grieg

Night on Bald Mountain,
Modest Mussorgsky

Ride of the Valkyries,
Richard Wagner

Illustrated by
Vaccaro Associates, Inc.

Cover by Dennis Durrell

Created and developed by
Lauren Keiser

D1133922

One sunny afternoon, Donald Duck took his three nephews to the amusement park. Huey, Dewey and Louie were very excited. They couldn't decide what to do first.

"Let's go on the merry-go-round!" Huey shouted.

"I want some ice cream," Dewey said.

"How about the roller coaster?" yelled Louie.

"Just a minute!" shouted Donald Duck. "Let's try that first."
He pointed to a dark, stone castle. The sign read "HAUNTED HOUSE."

"The Haunted House?" squeaked Dewey. "I-I-I don't know..."

"Yeah, that's too scary for me," Louie said.

"Aw, come on," said Donald. "There's nothing to be afraid of."

"Well, OK, Uncle Donald," said Huey. "If you say so."

Once they were inside, the wooden door slammed shut with a loud THUD!
The only light came from a candle flickering in the corner of the room.
It was damp and cold.

"Uh, maybe we should go back outside," Dewey said, looking around.
"It's kind of spooky in here."

I think my nephews are really scared, Donald said to himself.
Heh-Heh, this is going to be fun.

"Outside? Phooey!" Donald said. "I'm no chicken. Let me go first."

They walked into a large room. An orchestra was playing
and everyone was dancing.

"See? I told you it wasn't scary," Donald said, pointing to the couples twirling
around the dance floor.

Suddenly a trap door opened up and Donald fell through the floor to the cellar below. Huey, Dewey and Louie didn't notice.

"Look at those monsters!" Louie said. "And the skeletons playing the violins!"

Donald Duck was very surprised to find himself down in the dark cellar of the Haunted House. He jumped up when he felt something move right next to him.

"What was that?" Donald shouted. "Who are you? You don't scare me!"

My nephews must be terrified without me, Donald thought. *I should go find them.*

Meanwhile Huey, Dewey and Louie were having some fun in the Hall of Mirrors.

"Hey, look at me," Huey said laughing, "I'm ten feet tall!"

"Well, look at me," Dewey giggled, "I look like a snake!"

Louie said, "Has anyone seen Uncle Donald? He'd like this room."

Donald ran up the stairs as fast as his webbed feet could carry him. Finally, at the top of the stairs he saw a door. Donald pulled it open and ran inside. He was in a maze of endless hallways. He ran up and down, calling for help, but he couldn't find his way out.

"Look, there's Uncle Donald," Louie said, pointing. "What is he doing?" "Who knows, but he looks like he's having fun," Huey said. "Come on, let's go."

Donald was starting to lose his patience. Every time he opened a door to get out, there was another hallway. Creepy things kept flying over his head and jumping out at him. He sat down on a bench to take a short rest.

"Huey, Dewey, Louie," Donald called. "Don't be afraid, I'm coming."

All of a sudden, the bench lurched forward.
It started to roll down a steep hill. Faster and faster
it plunged into the darkness. Donald started to scream.

Huey, Dewey and Louie were far away— in the Dining Room of Doom.

"These guys look really hungry," Huey whispered.

"Yeah, and I think we're lunch!" giggled Dewey. "Let's get out of here!"

The boys climbed the stairs to the room above.
They sat down on a bench to rest.
It started to move.

The bench was climbing and climbing up a steep track.
At the top, the lights went out. They started to roll down the track.
Huey, Dewey and Louie held on tight as they flew through the darkness.

"Wow, this is neat, huh fellas?"
Huey shouted.

"Yeah, the best!" Dewey agreed.

"Hey, wasn't that Uncle Donald?" Louie asked, looking back.

Donald Duck was also flying up and down the
tracks. He didn't seem to be as happy as his nephews.

The roller coaster came to a screeching halt at the back door of the Haunted House.
Huey, Dewey and Louie jumped out.

"That was great!" Dewey said. "I'm glad Uncle Donald told us not to be afraid."

"Where is he, anyway?" Huey asked.

"Look!" Louie yelled.

Huey, Dewey and Louie ran to meet their uncle.

"What happened to you, Uncle Donald?" Huey said, laughing.
"You look like you've just seen a ghost!"

"Ghost! What ghost? I'm not afraid." Donald yelled.

"What do you want to do next, Uncle Donald?" Dewey asked.
"We could get hot dogs, or maybe go on the ferris wheel, or. . ."

"Or. . .we could go back in the Haunted House!" Louie shouted.

Donald Duck looked at his nephews and said, "Aw, that's kids' stuff.
Why don't we just go home."